The Best World Book Week Ever

Written By
Sarah Oliver

Illustrated By
Scott Wells

First published 2017
by Rowanvale Books Ltd
The Gate
Keppoch Street
Roath
Cardiff
CF24 3JW
www.rowanvalebooks.com
Library Cataloguing in Publication Data.
A catalogue record for this book is available from the British Library.

Dedicated with love to Lizzy, Lily, Eden, Codie and Joelan.

A big thank you to my sister Liz, for helping to edit the story, and Scott, for bringing Danny and his classmates to life.

This book couldn't have been written without the help of children from the following schools. They are passionate about reading, and were bursting with ideas during our writing workshops:

Adswood Primary School, Stockport (Y5 and Y6)

Cambridge Road Primary School, Ellesmere Port (Y5 and Y6)

St Mary's Roman Catholic Primary School, Swinton (Y5)

We have hidden a bookworm on every page! Can you find him?

There are lots of bananas too – how many can you count?

Danny loves reading.

He likes reading with his family.

He likes reading
with his friends.

He likes reading
by himself.

He reads all the time.

He only stops when it is time for sleep.

This week is special.
It is World Book Week!

On Monday, there is a book quiz.

Wilson Warriors   12 points

Dahl Dreamers   13 points

Danny and his class go hunting for bears,

and enjoy feeding caterpillars.

On Tuesday, they visit a library.

They choose a
hundred books.

and Danny and his friends
act out her story.

They have fun writing
a book together.

On Thursday, they have a tea party with special guests.

Everyone puts on their pyjamas

and pretends it is bed time.

On Friday, it is time to celebrate

with a
special parade.

The best World Book Week might have come to an end...

but there's always next year to look forward to!

The End.

Author Profile

Sarah Oliver is from Widnes in Cheshire. She's written over twenty books, and is best known for her Justin Bieber, Miley Cyrus, One Direction and Robert Pattinson biographies. Her books include the Sunday Times best-selling One Direction A-Z and Taylor Swift: Everything has Changed.

Sarah has also written books about superheroes and villains, how to be a successful rugby player, and a guide to the Hobbit movies. In her spare time, she enjoys family days out with her husband Jon and their two daughters, Lizzy and Lily. Sarah is a Christian and teaches a Sunday school class in her church. In September 2017, Sarah became the patron of Hand on Heart, a charity that saves lives by placing defibrillators in schools.

To find out more about Sarah, or to book her for an author talk in your school or library, please visit www.saraholiverauthor.co.uk. You can also get in touch with Sarah via twitter - @SarahOliverAtoZ.

Publisher Information

Rowanvale Books provides publishing services to independent authors, writers and poets all over the globe. We deliver a personal, honest and efficient service that allows authors to see their work published, while remaining in control of the process and retaining their creativity. By making publishing services available to authors in a cost-effective and ethical way, we at Rowanvale Books hope to ensure that the local, national and international community benefits from a steady stream of good quality literature.

For more information about us, our authors or our publications, please get in touch.
www.rowanvalebooks.com
info@rowanvalebooks.com